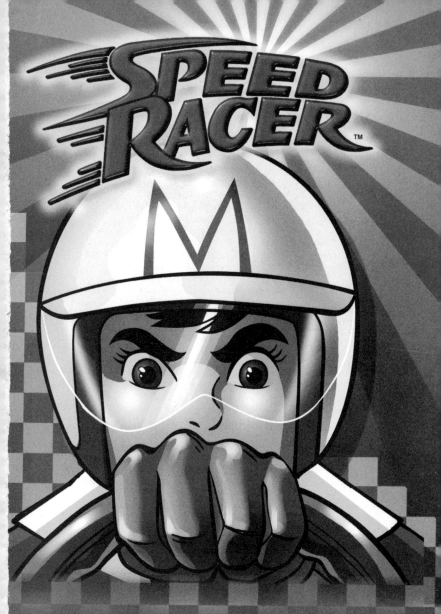

The Great Plan

GROSSET & DUNLAP
Published by the Penguin Group
Penguin Group (USA) Inc., 375 Hudson Street,
New York, New York 10014, USA
Penguin Group (Canada), 90 Eglinton Avenue East,
Suite 700, Toronto, Ontario M4P 2Y3, Canada
(a division of Pearson Penguin Canada Inc.)
Penguin Books Ltd., 80 Strand, London WC2R 0RL, England
Penguin Group Ireland, 25 St. Stephen's Green, Dublin 2, Ireland
(a division of Penguin Books Ltd.)
Penguin Group (Australia), 250 Camberwell Road,
Camberwell, Victoria 3124, Australia
(a division of Pearson Australia Group Pty. Ltd.)
Penguin Books India Pvt. Ltd., 11 Community Centre,
Panchsheel Park, New Delhi—110 017, India
Penguin Group (NZ), 67 Apollo Drive, Rosedale,
North Shore 0745, Auckland, New Zealand
(a division of Pearson New Zealand Ltd.)
Penguin Books (South Africa) (Pty.) Ltd., 24 Sturdee Avenue,
Rosebank, Johannesburg 2196, South Africa

Penguin Books Ltd., Registered Offices:
80 Strand, London WC2R 0RL, England

www.speedracer.com

Designed by Michelle Martinez Design, Inc.

Library of Congress Cataloging-in-Publication Data is available.

ISBN 978-0-448-44804-6   10 9 8 7 6 5 4 3 2

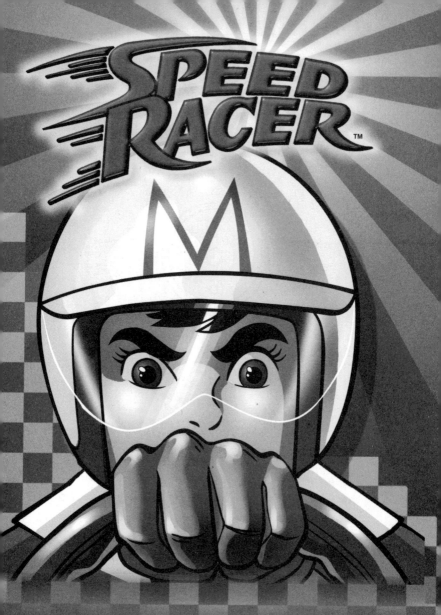

SPEED RACER™

The Great Plan

by Chase Wheeler   Grosset & Dunlap

The Marvels of the Mach 5

The Mach 5 is one of the most
powerful and amazing racing cars in
the world. Pops Racer designed the Mach 5
with features you won't see on any other car.
All of the features can be controlled by
buttons on the steering wheel.

(A) This button releases powerful jacks to boost the car so Sparky, the mechanic, can quickly make any necessary repairs or adjustments.

(B) Press this button and the Mach 5 sprouts special grip tires for traction over any terrain. At the same time, an incredible 5,000 torque of horsepower is distributed equally to each wheel by auxiliary engines.

(C) For use when Speed Racer has to race over heavily wooded terrain, powerful rotary saws protrude from the front of the Mach 5 to slash and cut any and all obstacles.

(D) Pressing the D button releases a powerful deflector that seals the cockpit into an air-conditioned, crash and bulletproof, watertight chamber. Inside it, Speed Racer is completely isolated and shielded.

(E) The button for special illumination allows Speed Racer to see much farther and more clearly than with ordinary headlights. It's invaluable in some of the weird and dangerous places he races the Mach 5.

(F) Press this button when the Mach 5 is underwater. First the cockpit is supplied with oxygen, then a periscope is raised to scan the surface of the water. Everything that is seen is relayed down to the cockpit by television.

(G) This releases a homing robot from the front of the car. The homing robot can carry pictures or tape-recorded messages to anyone or anywhere Speed Racer wants.

Speed Racer gripped the wheel as he raced around the track. A pack of cars led the race up ahead, but Speed wasn't worried.

He was driving the Mach 5. His dad, Pops Racer, had designed the Mach 5 to be the ultimate racing machine. The sleek white car could accelerate in the blink of an eye. It could handle sharp curves with ease. In the Mach 5, Speed felt like he could take on any course and win every race.

This was only a practice race. Pops Racer was an engineer for SRE Industries, one of the top race car companies in the world. It was his job to design faster, safer race cars. The race around the company track was one way the engineers tested the cars.

Speed didn't care if it was just practice. He wanted to win.

Speed stepped on the gas. He swerved in and out of the lanes, passing cars as he zipped by. The Mach 5's powerful engine buzzed in his ears as he roared down the track.

Now only a bright yellow car stood between Speed and victory. The track took a tight turn to the left. Speed zoomed even faster. He made the difficult turn, easily passing the yellow car. A cloud of dust kicked up behind his wheels. The finish line was in his sight . . .

"The Mach 5 wins!"

The guys in the SRE pit crew cheered and waved their arms. They all wore yellow uniforms and yellow caps with red brims. Speed slowed the Mach 5 to a stop as the pit crew gathered around him.

"What a race, Speed!" said Slim, a tall, thin mechanic wearing glasses. "You were fantastic!"

"Someday you'll be champion of the world," said Hank, a short mechanic with a friendly face.

"Nobody can beat you!" added a chubby mechanic named Mac.

Speed took off his racing helmet and goggles. His blue eyes were shining with excitement. Two

cars from the race pulled up alongside Speed, their tires screeching.

"That was a good race, Speed," said a driver in a blue car.

"You're the best driver I've ever seen, Speed," said the driver of the yellow car.

Speed ran a hand through his dark brown hair. "Thanks!" he replied, smiling.

Otto, the pit crew boss, walked up. He wore a red and white jacket. He was in charge of all the drivers who worked for SRE. "How'd you like to join my team as a professional racer?" he asked.

Speed's grin faded. "Uh, I don't know."

Slim put an arm around Speed's shoulder. "Speed, you can race with all of us in the Grand Prix!"

"I wish I could," Speed said sadly. He hopped out of the car and rested his arms on the hood. "But Pops doesn't want me to become a professional racer."

Speed sighed. He didn't think he would ever understand Pops. His dad lived and breathed race cars. Speed was practically born with racing fuel in his veins. So why wouldn't Pops let him become a pro?

"Your father's a top engineer working for this company," Otto pointed out. "Maybe he'll change his mind if we ask him."

"I doubt it," Speed said. He knew Pops. His dad could be really stubborn when he wanted to.

Speed tucked his hands in his pockets and started to walk off the track, his shoulders slumped. Slim, Otto, and Hank followed him, grabbing his arms.

"Don't give up, Speed!" Hank said.

"I want to be a professional racer," Speed replied. "I want to be the top champion. I want

that more than anything in the world!"

Otto nodded. "You're a fast and skillful driver, Speed. I think you have a good chance of realizing your ambition. Just stick to it."

"Thanks," Speed said, smiling again. "Don't worry about that."

Slim patted the Mach 5. "You can't lose with this amazing car," he said. "It can do everything."

"It's your father's masterpiece," Hank added. "You should be proud of him!"

"Oh, I am!" Speed replied. "And right now he's working on making it better with an even faster engine."

There was only one thing to do. Speed would have to convince Pops. He couldn't give up—no matter what.

Pops Racer stood in front of his board members at SRE Industries. The board members sat around a long table, staring at Pops. Pops Racer didn't look anything like the other men in the room. They were all small, thin, and wore expensive suits. Pops was a big, burly man with a thick brown mustache. Instead of a suit, he wore a red work shirt.

Pops was presenting the plans for the Mach 5's new engine. Sure, the Mach 5 was a great car, but Pops wanted to make it even better. To

do that, he had to impress the big boss, Mr. Wiggins. If Wiggins liked it, Pops could go ahead and build the engine. But if the big boss *didn't* like it, Pops's dream of improving the Mach 5 would be dashed.

Another man might have been nervous. Not Pops. He had faced tougher guys than Mr. Wiggins in the ring, back when he was a professional wrestler. Besides, Pops was talking about the Mach 5, the greatest race car in the world. Anyone could see that his plans for the car were brilliant.

"This is a model of the latest engine I have designed," Pops explained. He pointed to a steel mock-up of the engine behind him. It wasn't a working engine, but it would give the board members a picture of what he was doing.

"It will have more horsepower than any other car engine of its size," Pops continued. "Using the latest metals, fuels, and ignition systems, I can succeed in boosting the rpm to thirty thousand."

Pops grinned. With wheels that moved that fast, the Mach 5 would be unbeatable!

The board members couldn't believe what they were hearing.

"Thirty thousand?" one of the men asked. "If I didn't believe you, I'd say it was unbelievable!"

"I've worked on it for over a year," Pops said proudly. He held up his blueprints. "I hope you'll give me the go-ahead to actually build an engine according to this plan here."

Mr. Wiggins looked impressed. But not Mr. Van Ruffle, the chief engineer. His face turned red and he thumped his fist on the table.

"Don't waste time rebuilding it!" he bellowed.

Pops looked confused. "What? You haven't heard the rest of my plans for the Mach 5."

Mr. Van Ruffle stood up. "I've heard enough, Mr. Racer!" he said angrily. "I don't believe your plan can work!"

Pops was furious. "What do you know, Van Ruffle? Nothing! That's what."

Pops turned to Mr. Wiggins. "Mr. President, all I ask is that you develop my plans and give the car a try," he pleaded.

Mr. Wiggins looked at Pops through his wire-rimmed glasses. "I can't do that without the unanimous agreement of this board," he said. Pops groaned. The board included Mr. Van Ruffle.

"If the car turns out to be a failure, do you think this company should have to pay for your incompetence?" Van Ruffle asked Pops.

Pops couldn't take it anymore. The plans for the new engine were pure genius. He wasn't going to beg a bunch of businessmen who cared more about money than genius. *They* should be begging *him*.

"All right. You've had your chance," Pops said. He rolled up his blueprints and put them in his briefcase. "I'm not going to ask you for another. I quit!"

"I'm glad to see you leave, Mr. Racer," Van Ruffle called after him. "Good riddance!"

Pops stomped toward the door. "I'll rebuild

the Mach 5 myself and prove my design will work!" he huffed.

"We'll see! We'll see!" Mr. Van Ruffle called after him. Pops heard his sinister chuckle as he slammed the door behind him.

Speed picked up Pops in the Mach 5. Pops sat in the passenger seat, clutching his briefcase on his lap. The sky overhead was clear and blue as they drove through the mountain pass. But the nice weather was no match for Pops's mood. He was still pretty steamed about what had happened in the boardroom.

"Gee, Pops, maybe you shouldn't have quit your job," Speed said when he heard the story.

"I wouldn't have if they had let me rebuild the car," Pops grumbled.

"Why wouldn't they give you the go-ahead?" Speed asked. "After all the work you put into the plan?"

"One of the board members was jealous and didn't even want to look at my designs," Pops explained. "The board wouldn't give me the go-ahead. So I blew up."

Speed frowned. Pops was mad at the whole racing world. This was *definitely* not a good time to ask him about going pro.

"I'm going to forget about driving on a team," Speed muttered.

"What?" Pops asked.

"Nothing, Pops," Speed sighed.

"Maybe I'm wrong about rebuilding the Mach 5," Pops went on. "Maybe Van Ruffle is right. Maybe it would be a failure."

"It also might turn out to be the best racing car in the world," Speed pointed out.

That got Pops thinking, just like Speed knew it would. One good thing about Pops being stubborn was that he never gave up, even when things got tough.

The Mach 5 rounded a bend. Speed didn't notice, but a group of men on motorcycles sat on a hill, watching them pass. They revved their engines.

The bikers zoomed down the hill in hot pursuit of the Mach 5. Their red motorcycles gleamed in the sunlight. Now Speed saw them approach in his rearview mirror. Each bike had

silver lightning bolts painted on the side. They quickly surrounded the Mach 5.

Pops shook his briefcase at them. "Are you boys trying to take up the whole road?" he complained.

Then one of the bikers grabbed the briefcase right out of Pops's hand!

"Come back here! Come back!" Pops yelled.

Speed tried to catch up to the biker, but the other bikers zoomed in front of him, blocking his way. The biker with the briefcase turned his head.

"Thanks for the plans, Pops!" he cried.

Then he sped ahead.

"Give those plans back!" Pops yelled.

"You won't get away with them!" shouted Speed.

Pops turned to Speed. "How can we stop them?"

Speed thought quickly. He didn't want to slam the Mach 5 into the bikers. There had to be another way.

Speed stepped on the gas. He pulled the Mach 5 right up next to the biker with the briefcase.

"Pops, take the wheel!" Speed said. He stood up in the seat.

"No, Speed!" Pops cried. But it was too late to try and stop his son.

Speed jumped out of the Mach 5. He landed on the seat behind the biker. He grabbed the biker around the neck.

"Now give me those plans!" Speed said.

The bike began to swerve crazily along the road.

"Let me go! We'll crash! What are you doing?" shrieked the biker.

Speed didn't loosen his grip. "I want those plans back!"

The biker threw the briefcase to another member of the gang riding next to him.

"You take them!" he said.

The other biker laughed. "Bye-bye and thanks!"

"Come back here!" Speed yelled. "Those plans don't belong to you. Stop—or I'll stop you!"

The biker looked nervously over his shoulder. Speed jumped through the air and landed on the back of the second bike. He wrapped his arms around the biker's helmet.

"Hey, I can't see! Let go!" the biker yelled. Another biker rode up next to him. "Take it!"

The third biker zoomed ahead into a tunnel. Speed hung on to the second biker's back. The biker could barely keep the motorcycle under control.

When they came through the tunnel, the road took a sharp curve. The biker careened

toward a metal guardrail. Speed jumped off the bike just in time.

Crash! The bike slammed into the metal rail. Speed was glad he wasn't on it. But he was frustrated, too. The biker with the plans was escaping.

Then Speed heard a sound overhead. He ran out of the tunnel and saw a small gray helicopter in the sky.

"It's Trixie!" Speed cried.

Speed's girlfriend, Trixie, was full of surprises. Some people might see her pretty face and stylish clothes and think she was a fashion model. But Trixie had more skills than a secret agent, and flying a helicopter was one of them.

Another one of her skills was being able to sense when Speed needed help. He was glad to see her now. He waved his arms in the air. Then he remembered his radio. He and Trixie were always tuned to the same frequency so they could contact each other in emergencies.

"Hey, Trixie! I'm down here!" he yelled into the radio transceiver he held in his hand. "Some motorcycles are driving down the road. See if you can catch them. They stole Pops's plans for the Mach 5!"

"I'm going. I'll find them," Trixie promised.

Trixie flew off in the helicopter.

Then Speed heard shouts from inside the tunnel.

"Pops!" he cried. He quickly ran back into the tunnel.

Pops had steered the Mach 5 across the road, blocking the tunnel exit. Some of the bikers had

stayed by Pops and the Mach 5, trying to prevent Pops from helping Speed. But Pops had turned the tables on them. The bikers were trapped in the tunnel now. They stopped their bikes and jumped off to face Pops.

That's when Pops's wrestling moves came in handy.

Slam! Pops threw one biker to the ground.

Bam! Pops caught another biker in a headlock.

Wham! Pops hoisted another biker onto his shoulders. Then he hurled him to the ground!

The bikers groaned and struggled to their feet. Pops laughed. But he let down his guard too soon. Speed ran in just in time to see one of the bikers conk Pops over the head with a wrench. Pops moaned and fell to the ground.

The bikers surrounded Pops, ready to get their revenge. Speed tapped one of them on the shoulder.

"Hi," Speed said cheerfully.

The biker lunged for him, but Speed dodged
out of the way.

"Ow!" The biker collided with the concrete
wall of the tunnel.

Another biker ran toward Speed. Speed
jumped up, then wrapped his legs around the
goon's neck. They landed on the floor.

Pops opened his eyes and tried to sit up.
"That's the way, Speed. You're a chip off the old
block!" he cheered. "Show them they can't fool
with the Racers!"

Speed ran to Pops's side and helped him up.
They both jumped in the Mach 5.

"Let's see if Trixie found those guys," Speed said as he tried to catch his breath.

They zoomed down the highway. They spotted Trixie's helicopter just down the road. She was chasing one of the bikers—the one who held the briefcase!

Trixie flew the copter right over the biker's head. The startled goon lost control of the bike. He veered off the side of the road and broke through the guardrail. The briefcase flew out of his hands.

The Mach 5 squealed to a stop. Speed reached down and picked up the briefcase. As he bent down, he saw that the guardrail had ripped the goon's motorcycle in half. He was riding down the mountain on one wheel, looking like a clown on a unicycle.

Trixie contacted Speed on the walkie-talkie.

"Tell Pops next time he shouldn't give away his plans so easily," she teased.

"Don't worry, Trixie," Pops replied. "These

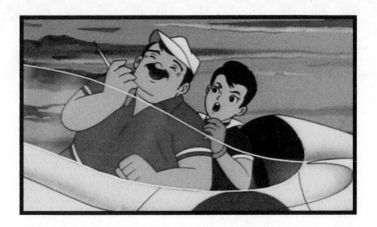

plans for the Mach 5 are the most valuable thing
we've got."

"To me, Speed's more valuable," Trixie
answered.

Pops laughed. Speed revved the engine once
more, and they sped toward home.

Speed's mom had dinner waiting for Pops and Speed when they got home. She was happy to see them, as always, but the news that Pops had quit his job worried her.

Speed's little brother, Spritle, was more worried about dessert. His pet chimpanzee, Chim Chim, was eating all of the cookies!

"Save some for me!" Spritle said.

"*Eek!*" said Chim Chim. He reached out and

grabbed another cookie off the plate.

Mom Racer made cups of tea for Pops and Speed. But Pops was too worried to enjoy it. He paced back and forth across the kitchen.

"Somebody tried to steal the plans, so that must mean they're valuable, right?" he wondered.

Mom had other things on her mind. "Yes, but now that you've quit your job, you won't know what to do with yourself," she said with a twinkle in her eyes. Her eyes were as green as the dress she wore. "I know how you like to keep busy. How about remodeling my kitchen, rebuilding the garage, and planting some shrubbery?"

"Hey, I've got a groovy idea, Pops," Speed said. "I'll help you with everything."

"Okay, but first I'm going to work on remodeling the Mach 5 myself," Pops said. "I'll prove to the suits down at the factory that these plans are genius."

"But where will you get the money for the

parts you need to rebuild the car?" Mom asked.

Pops frowned. "Where *am* I going to get that money?"

Spritle turned up the radio in the next room. He and Chim Chim began to dance. But Pops was feeling too worried about the money he needed to have fun.

"Quiet!" he bellowed.

"Waaaaah!" Spritle started to cry. Then Mom came out of the kitchen.

"Here, Spritle, I just baked a new batch of cookies," she said. She held the cookie plate out to him.

Spritle stopped crying. He reached out to grab a cookie, but Chim Chim ran up and snatched the plate right out of Mom's hands.

"Waaaah!" Spritle started to bawl again.

Pops groaned.

Everyone left the dinner table wondering how Pops was going to find the money to build his engine. Speed thought about Pops's problem all night long. When he went to bed, he stared out of the window at the starry sky.

Speed's biggest dream was to become a pro racer. But right now, his dad's dream was more important.

"I won't be a professional racer," he said to himself. "Instead I'll go to work. I'll earn enough money so Pops will be able to rebuild the Mach 5."

Across town, the same stars shone down on Mr. Van Ruffle's house. The chief engineer was yelling at a bunch of goons—the bikers who

had ambushed Speed and Pops earlier that day! They were all bruised and bandaged from their encounter with the Racers.

"You stoneheads! Don't tell me you're sorry!" Van Ruffle fumed. He had hired them to steal the plans from Pops Racer, and they had failed him.

"But we *are* sorry, Mr. Van Ruffle," said one of the goons. "Speed's strong and he got help from someone in a helicopter."

"Don't give me excuses!" Van Ruffle yelled.

A man in a trench coat stepped out of the shadows. He wore dark sunglasses, and a thin mustache covered his even thinner lips.

"I figured those guys would botch the job, and they did," the stranger said. "Give me five thousand clams and I'll get the plans."

"Five thousand dollars? You, sir, must be kidding!" Van Ruffle said.

"Oh, no," said the man calmly. "Ace Ducey doesn't kid. If you want those plans, it'll cost you

five thousand clams. If you don't want them, forget it."

Van Ruffle gritted his teeth. Five thousand dollars was a lot of money. But he knew that Pops Racer really was a genius. He had only pretended to think the plans were a bad idea so he could steal them for himself. In the right hands, those plans could be worth millions.

"All right, it's a deal," he said.

Ace Ducey grinned sinisterly. "You'll have the plans for the Mach 5 before you can say 'Ace Ducey'," he promised.

The next morning Speed drove the Mach 5 across town to see his best friend, Sparky. Sparky was the same age as Speed, but he was one of the best auto mechanics around. He could tear an engine apart and put it back together in his sleep.

Speed found Sparky working underneath a classic car. Sparky spent most of his time with a wrench in his hand.

"Hiya, Sparky," Speed said.

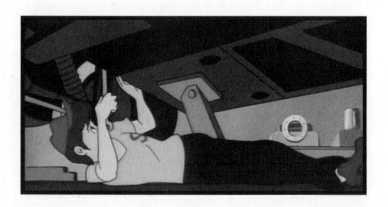

Sparky wheeled out from underneath the car. He wore a red cap over his light brown hair. A yellow T-shirt hung loosely on his skinny frame. He wiped his greasy hands on a rag.

"Oh, hi, Speed," Sparky said. "This is a great Jeep, isn't it?"

"Yeah," Speed said glumly. Normally he would have been excited about the old car, but today he had too much on his mind.

"The engine in there is a V8 with double overhead cams," Sparky went on. Then he noticed Speed's mood. "Hey, what's the matter? What are you looking so sad about?"

"I'm not going to try to become a pro racer," Speed said. He leaned against an oil drum and rested his chin in his hand. "I've got to find some other job."

"I know your dad's against it, but he'll come around," Sparky told him. "Don't give up."

"It's not that, Sparky. It's just that I need money, fast," Speed replied.

Sparky looked concerned. "You need money? What's going on?"

"I'm going to give it to Pops so he can build a super engine for the Mach 5," Speed explained.

Sparky nodded. The word about Pops quitting the factory had gotten around fast.

"I get it, Speed. But they told him at the factory that the engine wouldn't work," Sparky pointed out. "Anyway, read this before you do anything."

Sparky took a folded newspaper from his back pocket and gave it to Speed.

Speed read aloud from the paper. "A trial

race across Sword Mountain. Five thousand bucks to the winner."

Speed raised an eyebrow. Five thousand dollars would definitely help Pops build the engine.

"So why don't you enter it?" Sparky asked.

Speed frowned. "Pops would be furious if I did."

"But he's sure to forgive you when he realizes why you did it," Sparky pointed out. "Those five thousand clams should put a smile on his face."

Speed nodded. "You're right. I'll enter!"

Sparky grinned. "Now you're being smart, Speed. But Sword Mountain is going to be a tough course to drive. I'll fix the Mach 5 for climbing mountains."

"That'll be great," Speed said. "Thanks!"

Speed felt better already. All he had to do was win that race at Sword Mountain, and Pops's problems would be solved!

6

ACE DUCEY STRIKES

Back at the Racer house, Pops was working in his home office. He was bent over his drawing table, working out a formula, when . . .

Bam! A karate chop to the back of the neck knocked Pops out. When he came to, he found himself tied to a chair. A suspicious-looking man in a trench coat and sunglasses stood in front of him.

"Who are you?" Pops asked. He struggled to loosen the ropes that bound his wrists.

The man tipped his black hat toward Pops. "The name is Ace Ducey," he replied.

"And what do you want?" Pops asked angrily.

Ace grinned. "Your designs for improving the Mach 5."

Pops wished he wasn't tied to a chair. He was itching to take down Ace Ducey with a super body slam! But there was nothing he could do.

"You can't have them!" Pops cried.

"No problem," Ace said coolly. "I'm just going to help myself."

Ace began to search Pops's office. He opened drawers. He pulled out papers. Soon the office was a real mess—and Ace Ducey was angry. He pounded his fist into his hand and walked menacingly toward Pops.

"Where'd you hide those plans?" Ace asked. "Come on, where are they?"

Suddenly, there was a knock on the door. Speed walked in. He quickly realized Pops was in trouble.

"Pops!" Speed cried.

Ace Ducey had seen what Speed had done to Van Ruffle's goons. He didn't want a taste of that for himself. He quickly ran past Speed and out the door.

Speed wanted to chase after him, but he ran to untie Pops first.

"Who was that?" Speed asked, quickly working on the ropes.

"He came to get my plans for rebuilding the Mach 5," Pops grunted.

Speed untied the last rope. "We'll see about that," he said. Then he ran outside.

He was too late. Ace Ducey was nowhere to be seen.

Back in his office, Pops picked up a windshield from the floor. He carried it into a small room. Then he turned off the lights and turned on some special red lights.

The plan for the Mach 5 engine appeared on the windshield!

"Using invisible ink and drawing the designs on this windshield glass was a brilliant idea," Pops said. He chuckled at his own cleverness. "Nobody will think of looking here!"

7

CRASH TEST!

Speed knew he had to practice hard for the Sword Mountain race. Racing on the open road was a lot different than racing on a closed track. But first, Sparky had to do his magic.

Sparky gave the Mach 5 stronger shock absorbers so Speed would have a smoother, more controlled ride on the bumpy mountain trails. He raised the suspension of the Mach 5 by a few inches so Speed could drive over rocks without damaging the underside of the car.

After a few hours, Sparky wheeled out from underneath the carriage. He gave Speed the thumbs-up.

"Okay, the Mach 5 is now ready for mountain racing, Speed," Sparky announced.

"Great!" Speed replied. "Now I want to take it out on a road test."

Sparky and Speed headed to the racetrack. Speed did laps around the track while Sparky clocked him with a stopwatch. Speed zoomed around the track at lightning speed.

As Speed zipped by Sparky on his first lap, Sparky hit the button on the stopwatch. "Wow!" he exclaimed. "One minute, forty-five seconds. Great!"

Then Trixie pulled up to the track in her yellow convertible. Sprite and Chim Chim rode with her.

"Did you see that, Trixie?" Sparky asked. "He was really moving!"

Speed kept on down the track, handling the tight curves with ease. Then he noticed something in his rearview mirror. A red car with a number two painted on the hood was gaining on him. Speed gasped. This was supposed to be practice, not a race!

The car pulled up alongside Speed, and he saw the familiar face of a racer he knew all too well—Skull Duggery.

Sparky and the others spotted him, too.

"Hey, that car belongs to Duggery!" Sparky cried. "He races dirty."

Trixie frowned. Duggery thought he was the best racer around. He could smell competition a mile away. He'd probably shown up to prove he could beat Speed, she thought.

Speed and Duggery raced side by side along the track. First Speed took the lead, then Duggery sped in front of him. Then Speed took the lead again. They went back and forth until Duggery decided to change tactics.

Wham! Duggery slammed his car into the Mach 5. Speed tried to avoid him, but Duggery clung to him like grease to a mechanic.

"What's he doing to him?" Trixie cried.

Wham! Duggery slammed into the Mach 5.

Bam! Sparks flew as metal slammed into metal.

The attack sent the Mach 5 spinning off the track. Speed couldn't control it. The Mach 5 flipped on its side. Speed flew out of the car and landed facedown on the track.

Sparky jumped into Trixie's car, and they drove to Speed as fast as they could. They

hopped out and ran to Speed's side, crouching by his fallen body.

"Speed? Are you okay?" Sparky asked.

"Are you hurt?" Trixie asked, her eyes filled with worry.

"Speedy, talk to us, Speedy!" Spritle pleaded.

Speed opened his eyes and groaned. He propped himself up on his elbows. His whole body was sore, but otherwise, he felt okay.

Skull Duggery pulled up beside the wreck. Sparky turned on him, furious.

"What's the big idea, Duggery?" he asked,

shaking his fist in the air. "Now Speed won't be able to enter the Sword Mountain race!"

Duggery raised an eyebrow. "Speed's going to be a professional racer? How interesting."

Speed grabbed Sparky's arm. "You told him!" he said anxiously. He didn't want word getting around. What if Pops found out?

Sparky gave a sheepish shrug. "I didn't know it was a secret."

"I would have beaten you anyway, Speed, so you're lucky you won't be competing," Duggery sneered. "So long!"

Duggery waved as he drove away.

Speed gritted his teeth. He wanted to enter the race now more than anything. He had to prove to Duggery that he was no loser.

Trixie leaned over him. "You're planning to be in a professional race?" She sounded concerned.

Spritle shook his head. "Pops isn't going to like it!"

"He's not supposed to know. Don't tell him, Sprite," Speed said.

"He wants to win money so Pops can build a better engine for the Mach 5," Sparky explained.

Trixie's eyes widened. "Oh, I see."

"I won't tell Pops," Spritle promised. Then he put his hand over Chim Chim's mouth. "And don't you tell him either, Chim Chim!"

Everyone laughed. Speed was starting to feel better already.

Now all they had to do was fix the Mach 5— and win the race at Sword Mountain!

Sparky and Speed spent hours getting the Mach 5 fixed and ready for the race. They replaced a cracked radiator and banged out dents in the doors. Spritle and Chim Chim watched, handing Sparky tools when he needed them.

"Almost done," Sparky said. "We just need to figure out what to do about the broken windshield. And we've got to put some finishing touches on the engine."

Sparky and Chim Chim looked at each other and grinned. Then they quietly slipped out.

Speed went to work on the engine, tightening some loose coils and wires. Then he closed the hood of the Mach 5.

Sparky came strolling through the garage, whistling and rolling a brand-new tire.

Any ordinary car would have to be put on a

lift to raise it up so the new tire could go on. But thanks to Pops, changing tires on the Mach 5 was much easier.

Speed pressed the A button on the steering wheel. Four powerful jacks extended from the bottom of the car, lifting the Mach 5 above the ground.

"Put it on," Speed instructed.

Sparky used a wrench to tighten the lug nuts on the wheel. Then he nodded to Speed. "Okay!"

Next, Speed pressed the B button on the steering wheel. This released a special protective

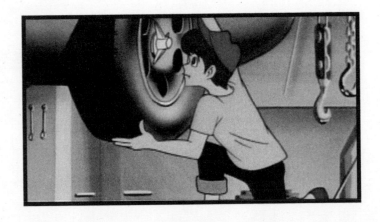

covering that wrapped around all four of the car's wheels.

Sparky grinned with pride. "Now the Mach 5 has Pops's special grip tire system for mountain areas. How can you lose?"

Then he frowned. "I forgot. We still don't have a windshield!"

The old windshield had shattered when Skull Duggery ran Speed off the road. Sparky could fix just about anything, but they'd need cash to replace the windshield—cash they didn't have.

"Let's forget about it, Sparky," Speed said. "I'll just have to race without any glass on the car."

But that idea worried Sparky. "Don't be foolish, Speed. You need the protection."

Speed glanced at the clock. They could probably dig up a used windshield in a junkyard, but that could take forever, and the race was going to start in an hour.

"There isn't time to go looking for one," Speed said anxiously.

"But you can't race without a windshield!" Sparky insisted.

Then Spritle and Chim Chim walked in, carrying a windshield!

"Look! We found a windshield!" Spritle announced with a grin.

Sparky slapped him on the back. "Nice going, Spritle!"

But Speed knew where that windshield had come from. He had seen it before.

"That belongs to Pops," Speed said.

"Don't worry about it, Speed," Spritle told him. "We'll take care of Pops!"

Spritle walked confidently out of the garage, swinging his arms. Chim Chim followed, swinging his arms the same way. Speed had to smile. With their red overalls and striped caps, Spritle and Chim Chim even dressed alike! Sometimes it felt like Speed had *two* little brothers.

Spritle found a phone in the office of the garage. He called Pops at home.

"Pops speaking!" he answered.

"Hi, Pops," Spritle said cheerfully. "Is it okay if Speed borrows your windshield for a little while?"

"Why does he want that?" Pops yelled. Chim Chim jumped at the sound of his loud voice. "Where is Speed right now, anyway?"

"He's going to race at Sword Mountain—" Spritle began. Then he cringed.

"Oh, no! I shouldn't have told Pops that!" he told Chim Chim.

Pops was fuming now. "He took my windshield, huh? Why, I—"

Spritle hung up the phone and shrugged. "I wonder what Pops is so sore about?"

Spritle and Chim Chim walked back into the garage.

"What did Pops say?" Speed asked.

"He was very excited that you're using the windshield," Spritle replied, not exactly telling the truth.

Speed shrugged. "Okay, Sparky. Let's get that windshield installed!"

Speed and Sparky picked up the glass and began to fit it into the Mach 5.

Back in his office, Pops was still fuming.

"I wrote all the designs in invisible ink on that windshield!" he fumed. "If that glass is broken, those plans will be gone forever!"

Pops heard a sound behind him. Ace Ducey was there—and he'd heard everything Pops had said.

"Clever of you to hide those designs on the windshield," Ace said. "It makes my job easier. To get them, all I have to do is take Speed's car."

"You'd better not!" Pops threatened. He lunged toward Ace, but the thug was ready for him.

Bam! Ace conked Pops on the head. Pops fell to the floor with a thud.

Ace snickered as he jumped on his motorcycle.

Speed Racer was not going to finish that race at Sword Mountain—not if Ace Ducey could help it!

When the Mach 5 was finished, Speed headed for Sword Mountain. The race would begin on a professional racetrack, then veer off to an off-road course.

Racing fans crowded the stands as the drivers lined up on foot for the race. They stood across the track, facing their cars. A bright blue sky shone overhead.

Speed got stuck standing next to Skull Duggery. Duggery wore a red uniform and helmet to match his car.

"I'm going to win this race, Speed, and those five thousand bucks will be mine," Duggery taunted.

"You better not count on them, Duggery," Speed responded.

Across the track, Sprite and Chim Chim

peeked out of the trunk of the Mach 5. Speed didn't know it, but his little brother and pet chimpanzee had stowed away! Spritle took after Pops and Speed—he loved a race. Just because he wasn't old enough to drive didn't mean he had to miss out on all of the excitement.

"This is going to be some ride, Chim Chim!" Spritle said. Then he quickly closed the trunk so they wouldn't be caught.

The announcer's voice blared from a loudspeaker. "All drivers stand by! When the flag is lowered, drivers will run to their cars and start. Racing positions on the track will be determined by quick starts and getaways. Get ready! The race will begin in exactly fifteen seconds!"

Speed got into position, his heart pumping. He couldn't wait for the race to start.

A man stepped out onto the track, holding a red flag above his head.

Bam! A shot rang out. The man lowered the flag. The race was on!

Speed charged across the track. He jumped into the Mach 5 a split second before Duggery hopped into his own race car. Speed and Duggery revved their engines and took off. They were the first to lead the pack.

Speed took the lead, but Duggery was right on his tail.

"Speed! Watch out for Duggery!" Sparky warned from the sidelines.

A racer in a yellow car tried to pass Duggery. Duggery smiled and steered right toward the car, forcing it off the track.

"*Aaaaah!*" the driver yelled as his car careened over the safety wall. Onlookers in the stands screamed and scrambled to get out of the way.

Wham! The car crashed into the stands. The shaken driver crawled out of the car as medics rushed to help him.

Duggery grinned. He wasn't going to let anyone come between him and Speed.

A driver in a blue car tried to pass Duggery.

Bam! Duggery slammed into the race car. The blue car spun out of control. The driver behind him couldn't stop in time, and the two cars collided.

Speed watched the action in his rearview mirror and frowned. There was no room in the sport for a dirty racer like Duggery.

The track opened up to the mountain road. The colorful stands gave way to a landscape of red rocks and dirt. Duggery caught up to Speed just as the road changed. The two kicked up red dust as they led the race, side by side.

Ace Ducey waited patiently down the road. He had gathered a small army of goons to help him steal the plans for the Mach 5. He and his men were all driving black race cars. They idled their engines, waiting for the right moment to strike.

Ace radioed his men. "Our target is car number five. We want its windshield."

Seconds later, Speed zoomed past. Ace and

his men drove onto the road and entered the race. The road was crowded with the other race cars.

"The other cars are in the way! Get rid of them!" Ace ordered his goons.

A sharp spike poked from the hubcap of each wheel on the black race cars. One of Ace's goons drove alongside a green race car. The smell of burning rubber filled the air as the spikes tore into the race car's tire.

The green car veered out of control. *Bam!* It crashed into another car, sending both cars spinning off of the road.

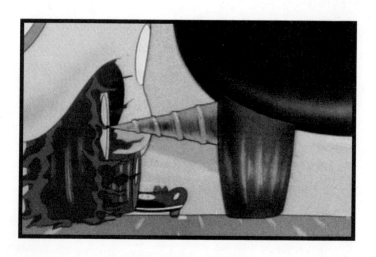

Two more cars sped up, and Ace's men struck using the same dirty trick.

Slash! Slash! The spikes ripped the tires on the two cars. The cars spun wildly out of control and smashed into the rocky mountainside.

Soon the road was a pile of burning, twisted metal. The drivers climbed out of their wrecked cars and shook their fists at the goons.

Duggery watched the attack in his mirror. "I don't know who's driving those new cars in the race, but they're looking for trouble," he muttered to himself. "I don't want any of them trying to wreck me."

Duggery swerved off the main road and headed down a dusty trail.

Spritle and Chim Chim heard all the commotion from their hiding place. They opened the trunk and peeked out to see a fleet of black cars advancing on the Mach 5.

"Look, Chim Chim, we're in for it!" Spritle cried.

Ace Ducey had exactly what he wanted. Speed was the only driver on the road now. He pulled up alongside Speed.

"You better do as I say, otherwise I'll smash you right off the course!" he called out over the roar of the engines.

The other black race cars surrounded Speed.

"All I want is your windshield. Give it to me or I promise you'll never reach the finish line!" Ace shouted.

Speed thought fast. He recognized Ace as the thug who'd tied up Pops, trying to steal the plans for the Mach 5.

There's only one reason they'd want this windshield, Speed realized. *I bet Pops hid the design on it.*

Well, there was no way he was going to let Ace Ducey get his hands on those plans!

"Come on! Take it off if you can!" Speed taunted.

"That kid's a fool!" Ace said angrily.

He sidled up next to the Mach 5, and Speed saw the sharp spikes protruding from Ace's wheels. He quickly steered out of the way.

They were on a rough stretch of road now. It twisted and turned like a snake. Guardrails were the only thing that could stop a car from falling down the steep cliffsides on either side of the road.

"Whoa!" Speed cried out. He expertly steered through the twists and turns. But Ace was right

on him. There was only one way to escape Ace.

Speed pressed the A button on the steering wheel. The hydraulic jacks lowered, then sent Speed soaring right over the guardrail!

Speed had escaped Ace. There was only one problem.

Now the Mach 5 was hurtling down the side of a rocky cliff!

The Mach 5 slammed into the rugged hillside. Speed quickly pulled back the jacks. The car careened crazily down the rough road. The wheels of the Mach 5 ground into rocky turf.

Speed didn't lose control. The bottom of the cliff ended at the bank of a stream. Speed steered the Mach 5 over a big log that crossed the stream. Then he sped off through a flat stretch of land at the bottom of a cliff.

Ace and his goons watched Speed from up on the main road. They knew they could never follow Speed off the trail like that. Their cars would be crushed.

"What a daredevil!" one of the goons cried.

"He made it, though!" said another.

Ace frowned. "Not for long!"

Speed drove across the dirt and back to the

main road. Except for Speed, it was deserted.

"No sign of Ace and his men," Speed said. "Good. I guess they've given up."

Speed drove on. The scene around him became greener as he drove through fields at the base of the mountain. Houses dotted the landscape here and there. The mountain peaks surrounded the valley, their tops covered with snow.

The sound of another engine drowned out the Mach 5's roar. But it wasn't a race car engine. It was a small biplane flying overhead.

The radio in the Mach 5 crackled.

"Trixie calling the Mach 5. Trixie calling the Mach 5." Trixie's voice came over the radio. "The designs are written on your windshield in invisible ink!"

"I know, Trixie," Speed replied. "Don't worry, I'll be careful. But I'm going to finish this race and win the money Pops needs."

"But Speed, those men aren't going to give up so easily," Trixie said anxiously. "They'll stop at nothing to get those designs. And if they don't get them, they'll make sure no one else does by getting rid of you and the Mach 5."

"I'll be all right, Trixie, I promise," he said. He looked up at her. "See you later!"

Trixie turned off the radio. "He's in danger. Doesn't he know it?"

She couldn't help worrying. As Trixie flew off, she wondered if there was some way she could help . . .

A feeling of pure energy coursed through Speed as he raced down the mountain road. He could see a group of race cars just up ahead.

That meant his little detour hadn't put him out of the race—not yet.

Speed stepped on the gas. He easily overtook the cars in front of him.

"Whee!" cried Spritle, still stowed away inside the trunk. "With Speed at the wheel, how can we lose the race? He'll win!"

The Mach 5 hit a bump in the road. Spritle and Chim Chim hit their heads on the roof of the trunk.

"Aaaah!" Spritle yelled, but Chim Chim quickly covered his mouth. After all, the last thing Speed needed was to find out they were stashed in the trunk!

Now that he wasn't worried about Ace and his goons, Speed had his mind on the race. He forged ahead. Another pack of cars led the race in front of him. Speed passed one car, then the next. As he approached the lead it was just as he feared—Skull Duggery's red car was in first place.

"I've got to pass that car!" Speed muttered.

Duggery saw the Mach 5 in his mirror.

"Uh-oh! The Mach 5!" Duggery said. "But Speed's not going to win this race, not if I can help it."

Duggery shifted gears as the road grew steeper. That didn't stop Speed. He was right on Duggery's tail now.

"I'll try to pass!" Speed said.

Speed sped up and tried to pass Duggery on the left. The road took a sharp turn. Duggery veered left at the same time, ramming his car into the Mach 5.

The encounter bumped the Mach 5 into the steel guardrail. A loud screech filled the air as metal scraped against metal. Spritle and Chim Chim bounced around in the trunk.

"I'll be glad when Speed gets on a straight road again," Spritle told Chim Chim. "This race is murder!"

Speed straightened out the Mach 5. He and

Duggery were side by side again. Then a cloud of dust appeared on the road in front of them. Speed gasped. The black race cars were heading straight for them!

"Here come Ace Ducey and his gang!" Speed yelled.

Speed and Duggery slammed on their brakes.

"Is there any way to avoid them?" Speed asked Duggery.

"Well, there's a road on the other side of that field," Duggery said, nodding toward the field next to them.

Speed nodded and took off, driving over the grass.

"He'll never make it!" Duggery said.

But Speed knew that tall grass was no problem for the Mach 5. He hit the C button on his steering wheel. Round rotor blades extended out from under the car. They spun quickly, chopping down the grass in front of the Mach 5. Once Duggery saw what Speed was doing, he turned off the road and followed the Mach 5's path.

Ace Ducey and his goons weren't worried.

"Lucky for us he went that way," Ace told his men over the radio. "In a few minutes he'll be a sitting duck. Let's go!"

The black race cars steered off the road and followed Speed and Duggery across the field. Blades of grass kicked up from the Mach 5. They flew past Duggery's car, and right into Ace's face!

"I don't mind somebody's dust, but this is ridiculous!" Ace complained.

The field emptied out onto a mountain pass. Two large cliffs rose up on either side of the narrow road. Speed and Duggery raced ahead of the black cars, but Ace's men were gaining fast.

Spritle and Chim Chim peered out from the trunk.

"This doesn't look good!" Spritle said, worried. "Speed better do something while he can!"

The road opened up to a wide canyon. Speed and Duggery were able to break away from the black cars.

It wasn't much of a lead, but it was enough for Trixie to spring into action. She had been following Speed the whole time. Now she swooped down from the sky in the biplane, nearly grazing the heads of the drivers. The goons gasped in surprise.

Trixie pressed a button in the cockpit, and a door in the bottom of the plane slid open. Several black canisters dropped out.

"*Aaaahhhh!* Bombs!" screamed one of Ace Ducey's thugs.

The canisters hit the ground and rolled,

releasing clouds of blue gas. The race cars skidded to a stop, and their riders raced out of the cars, searching for cover.

"Get down!" Ace yelled.

Ace's men dropped to the dirt and covered their heads, waiting for the explosion.

It never came.

"Huh?" Ace wondered.

The canisters continued to spit out clouds of smoke. Ace and his men coughed and wheezed.

"It was just a trick!" Ace said, stomping his foot. "They're only smoke flares!"

The men jumped back in their cars and continued to race after Speed. But Trixie wasn't about to give up. She kept hurling smoke flares in front of the cars. The thick blue smoke threw the drivers off course. The thugs screamed and stopped their cars. One skidded right to the edge of a cliff!

Ace had had enough. He took a road flare

gun from his car. Most drivers relied on the burst of bright fiery light when they needed to call for help. But Ace had something else in mind.

"I'll take care of this," Ace told his men.

Ace aimed the road flare right at the plane's engine.

Bam! The flare set the engine on fire. The plane quickly went up in flames. It wavered in the sky for a second, then crashed into the rocky mountainside.

Ace let out an evil laugh.

"Now we're even!" he called out.

Ace's cruel happiness didn't last long.

"Hey, look!" one of his thugs cried. He pointed to the sky.

Ace looked up to see Trixie floating safely to the ground on a yellow parachute. There wasn't a scratch on her.

Trixie grinned. "I've always wanted to find out what parachute jumping was like!"

Then she gasped. A team of black race cars

was speeding down the road below. When she landed, they'd be waiting there for her!

But there wasn't anything she could do about that now.

Speed had no idea Trixie was in trouble. He and Duggery raced down the canyon. They came to a fork in the road. A tall signpost held two signs. One sign pointed to a road on the left that was twenty-five miles long. The other pointed to a road on the right that was a shortcut—only fifteen miles long.

Duggery didn't hesitate. He quickly turned to the right.

"I'm taking the shortcut," Duggery said to himself. "It'll keep me away from Speed and those other guys."

Speed started to take the left turn, but stopped. He knew the shortcut was a bad idea.

"Duggery's heading for the volcanoes," Speed realized. He had studied a map of the area before the race, and he knew where that road led. "He'll smash up down in that area."

Speed raced after Duggery. Three volcanoes suddenly loomed before them. Thick gray smoke blew from each volcano.

"Duggery! Get out of here!" Speed yelled.

"Mind your own business!" Duggery shouted back.

The ground underneath them became rockier and bumpier with each spin of the wheel. The Mach 5 could handle it, but not Duggery's race car. One of his tires got stuck on a large rock. It spun wildly, then quickly broke free. This propelled Duggery's car over the rocks, toward the volcano.

"*Aaaaaaaaah!*" Duggery screamed as his car flipped over and over. It stopped right at the edge of one of the volcanoes, the nose of the car hanging over the edge.

The rocks under the wheels began to crumble and break. Speed skidded to a stop and ran to Duggery's car.

"Duggery!" he cried.

But his rival was not in the car.

He must have been thrown when his car flipped over, Speed realized. *But where is he?*

Speed peered over the rim of the volcano.

"Duggery! Where are you?" Speed called out. "Duggery! Aaaaaaah!"

The rock under Speed's boots broke, sending Speed tumbling into the volcano. He clawed at the volcano's walls with his hands, trying to stop his fall. He skidded to a stop on a narrow ledge.

Speed looked down. Lava bubbled down below in the center of the volcano. Fiery flames leaped up from the lava. Speed could feel the heat.

Then Speed heard a groan from below. Duggery was clutching on to a rock ledge a little below him.

"Looks like neither one of us is going to win those five thousand bucks," Duggery said. His voice was strained from the effort of hanging on. "We'll be lucky if we get out of this alive."

Duggery tried to pull himself up, but he didn't have the strength. Speed's mind raced as he tried to think of a plan.

If he hadn't been so stubborn, we wouldn't be down here, he thought. *I might be able to climb out, but I can't leave him trapped there. I've got to help him.*

The small ledge in Duggery's grasp began to break away from the volcano wall.

"The ledge is giving way!" Duggery yelled.

"Hang on! I'm coming!" Speed told him.

Speed carefully worked his way down the ledge until he was within Duggery's reach. He held out his right hand.

"Hang on to my hand. I'll try to pull you out of there," Speed directed him.

Duggery grabbed Speed's hand—just in time. The rock he had been holding broke away and tumbled into the boiling lava below. Duggery screamed in terror.

"Climb!" Speed ordered.

Duggery struggled to climb up to the ledge that held Speed. But he couldn't get a foothold.

"Come on!" Speed urged.

Duggery dug his boots into the rock, but the rock gave way.

"Aaaah!" Duggery screamed. Only Speed's strong grip kept him from falling. Sweat poured down Speed's face. His arm strained with Duggery's weight. But he didn't let go.

"Come on, we can make it together," Speed said through gritted teeth.

They climbed up the craggy volcano wall, digging their feet in whatever crack or crevice they could find. Speed pulled Duggery along the whole way. They finally reached the rim, just under Duggery's car.

With a sickening lurch, the whole edge of the rim gave way underneath them. They screamed and reached for the only thing they could—the axles of Duggery's wheels.

But the weight of the two racers was too much for the car. It started to tip over, ready to fall at any minute. If the car fell, Speed and Duggery would fall with it.

"I'm going to jump," Duggery said. "Follow me."

Duggery swung to the right and then let go of the car. He grabbed the edge of the volcano.

Speed followed. For a split second he was flying in midair, and his stomach dropped. Then his driving gloves gripped the volcano's rim. He pulled himself up next to Duggery. Speed was grateful to feel solid earth beneath his body.

"The only way we'll be able to get out of this area is if we both use the Mach 5," Duggery said.

They both looked toward Speed's car—and let out a sharp gasp.

Ace Ducey and his men had parked their race cars. Now they were running toward the Mach 5!

Ace and his goons quickly surrounded the Mach 5. Speed and Duggery raced to stop them.

"The plans we want are written in invisible ink on this windshield," Ace told his men, an evil grin on his face. He turned to Speed. "We're taking the Mach 5. Try to stop us and it will be too bad for her."

Ace pointed at Trixie, who was being held by one of his goons.

"How did you get here?" Speed asked.

"It's easy," Trixie said in her usual cheerful way. "Ace shot my plane with a road flare, so I jumped out and came down by parachute."

Road flare? Parachute? Speed was glad Trixie was all right—but now he was angrier with Ace Ducey than ever.

"Let her go!" Speed cried.

Ace ignored Speed. He nodded to his men. "We've got the plans, so now we can get rid of these troublemakers. We don't want anybody finding out how we got those plans."

Skull Duggery casually started to walk away.

"Hey, you! Hold it!" one of the thugs yelled.

Duggery turned his head. "I have nothing to do with this whole thing. I just want to get back in the race. So long."

Duggery kept walking.

"Stop him!" Ace yelled.

One of the goons charged at Duggery, tackling him to the ground.

Speed saw his chance to move. He aimed a karate chop at the chest of the nearest goon. The thug groaned and doubled over.

Speed ran for Trixie, but the goon holding her dragged her toward the Mach 5. Suddenly the bad guy screamed in pain. His hand flew to his face.

Someone was throwing rocks at Ace and his men!

"Who's throwing rocks? Come out of there!" Ace threatened.

Speed lunged at the goon holding Trixie, aiming a karate kick right at his knees. The man buckled over, and Trixie ran free. But another goon quickly grabbed her, and an army of thugs descended on Speed.

Meanwhile, Duggery jumped back on his feet—and he was angry. He grabbed the thug who had tackled him and flipped him.

Slam! The man's back thudded into the dirt.

Spritle and Chim Chim watched the rumble from the trunk of the Mach 5. Spritle held a slingshot and got ready to throw another rock. Then one of the goons spotted them. He growled angrily and stomped toward them.

Spritle stuck out his tongue. He and Chim Chim laughed. Then they closed the trunk.

The confused thug tapped the trunk of the car. Spritle and Chim Chim popped out, laughed, and then closed the trunk again.

The man tapped the trunk. Spritle and Chim Chim popped out. An excited Chim Chim climbed on top of the trunk. But the hood shut underneath him, leaving Spritle inside.

"Eek!" Chim Chim cried. The big goon grabbed him. Then he opened up the trunk and pulled out Spritle, grabbing him with his other hand.

"Our plan almost worked," Spritle said. "We got nearly all of them with the slingshot. Guess we'd better think of something else."

"Eek!" Chim Chim replied. He chomped down on the bad guy's hand.

The thug let out a shriek and dropped Chim Chim. Spritle chipped in by giving the guy a hard kick. He dropped Spritle, too. Then Spritle and Chim Chim took off running.

"Come back here, you little brats! Wait till I get my mittens on you!" the bad guy yelled.

Spritle and Chim Chim hid behind a big boulder. The man chased after them, but couldn't stop himself in time. He ran right into the rock!

The man's face turned bright red.

"Come back here!" he yelled.

He chased Spritle and Chim Chim around

and around the rock. The little guys were fast. They quickly jumped on top of another boulder. Spritle grabbed a rock.

Wham! The rock came down on the bad guy's head, and the bad guy went down.

Spritle and Chim Chim cheered.

"One more for us!" Spritle cried happily.

Back at the Mach 5, Speed and Duggery continued to fight the thugs.

Slam! Speed flipped one of the goons.

Bam! Speed pummeled another bad guy.

One of the thugs ran toward Duggery. Thinking quickly, Duggery picked up a rock and threw it at the man's feet. The thug tripped and then bumped his head into one of the black cars.

Spritle and Chim Chim happily jumped up and down. Chim Chim did a little flip.

"Hurray for Duggery! Hurray for Duggery!" Spritle cheered.

Then they saw someone running for them. The big bad guy who had chased them before had woken up.

"Just wait till I get you troublemakers!" he yelled.

Spritle and Chim Chim ran in a circle around him. They ran so fast that they hid right behind his legs. He didn't even know they were there. The thug had big muscles, but his brains were pretty puny.

"Where'd they go?" he asked.

Chim Chim jumped up on Spritle's shoulders. He gave the bad guy a push. He toppled over like a bowling pin.

"That makes two for us!" Spritle cried happily.

By now the ground was littered with Ace's men. Speed had taken care of most of them with karate chops. Duggery had taken down a few with some old-fashioned fighting, too.

Then the sound of a wailing siren filled the valley. Everyone stopped fighting and froze. The bad guys looked panicked.

"The police!" Ace yelled. "We better get out of here!"

While everyone was fighting, Spritle had hidden himself behind a rock. He blew into a toy siren that sounded exactly like a police car headed for the scene. He chuckled as the thugs fell for his trick and began to panic.

Trixie delivered a karate chop to the now distracted thug holding her. She ran to Speed's side.

"Speed! Are you all right?" she asked.

Speed nodded. "Are you?" he asked. But Speed never heard Trixie's answer. It was drowned out by the familiar sound of a powerful engine revving. Speed turned to see Ace Ducey drive off in the Mach 5!

Speed ran to a black race car. One of Ace's men blocked his path.

"I'm taking that car!" Speed told him. He

jumped up and knocked the goon over with a karate kick. Then he hopped in the black car and took off after Ace.

Ace looked in the rearview mirror and saw Speed trying to catch up to him. "Ha-ha! Now I've got the fastest car in the universe!" Ace gloated. "He'll never catch me now."

Speed stepped on the gas pedal of the black race car. The car's wimpy engine barely picked up speed.

"What kind of cheap car is this?" Speed complained. "It doesn't move fast enough to catch the Mach 5."

Speed could hear Ace's evil laugh as the goon

sped even farther away in the Mach 5.

"This car has got everything," Ace said to himself. "Including plans on the windshield for an even better engine!" he said. That made him start laughing even harder. He tapped his boot on the floor of the car. His foot accidentally hit a button. The Mach 5's hood flipped up, blocking his vision.

"How do I work this car?" Ace asked frantically.

Ace started freaking out. He took his foot off the gas, and the car slowed down. Then he started pressing buttons on the steering wheel, hoping to lower the hood.

Instead, he lowered the hydraulic jacks. The Mach 5 began to hop up and down.

Thanks to Ace's confusion, Speed was easily able to catch up.

"I've caught up with him, but how do I get him to stop?" Speed wondered out loud.

Speed pulled up alongside Ace in the Mach 5. He stood up in the driver's seat. With a cry, he leaped into the Mach 5!

The black race car spun out of control. It smashed through a guardrail and crashed into the embankment below, exploding in flames.

Speed and Ace grappled for control of the steering wheel. Speed tried to pry Ace's hands off of the wheel, but he wouldn't budge.

The car veered off the road now. Speed yanked Ace off of the wheel, but the villain toppled over, pulling Speed with him. Ace and Speed wrestled on the trunk of the Mach 5. The driverless car zoomed toward the guardrail, about to crash!

Then Ace's boot knocked into the A button. The hydraulic jacks kicked in again. The car bounced over the guardrail and landed on a flat ledge below the road. Now the Mach 5 zigzagged across the grass, headed right for the edge of a steep cliff!

Speed took off his helmet and conked Ace over the head. He pushed him out of the car and into the grass. Then he jumped into the driver's seat and slammed on the brakes.

The Mach 5 spun into a 360, kicking up a cloud of dust. It stopped inches away from the edge of the cliff.

Speed leaned against the steering wheel, relieved. But his troubles weren't over yet. Ace Ducey stood in front of him. He had a menacing grin on his face and a small boulder in his hands.

"You are a tough kid, Speed, but you are no match for Ace Ducey!" the villain cried.

Speed had to think quickly. If Ace chucked that boulder at the Mach 5, the car would go tumbling over the ledge.

"Get out of the car, Speed," Ace said. "Those plans belong to me."

I can't let him get the designs that Pops wrote on the windshield. I can't! Speed thought.

Then he knew what he had to do.

Crash! Speed smashed his helmet into the windshield, shattering it. Ace gasped in horror.

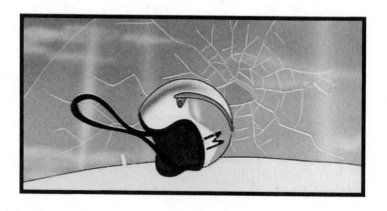

"You've smashed the designs!" he wailed.

Ace was in shock, and now Speed had the advantage. He swung himself out of the car, kicking Ace's wrists so that Ace had to drop the boulder. The kick was so strong that it sent Ace somersaulting over the edge of the cliff.

Speed peered over the cliff. Ace had landed in a puddle of mud below. He was all right—but he wasn't going to be chasing Speed for a while.

Then Speed heard the roar of an engine. He turned to see Skull Duggery speeding down the road, riding in his red race car once more.

"I better get back into the race—and fast!" Speed realized.

Speed jumped in the Mach 5 and sped after Duggery. As he raced down the mountain road, he realized he was in luck. The rest of the race cars in the Sword Mountain race were just up ahead. He was back on track.

Behind him, Sparky tried to catch up in his little yellow car. Trixie had radioed for help from the volcano, and Sparky had picked up Trixie, Spritle, and Chim Chim. Now they hurried back toward the racetrack.

"Go, Speed, go!" Spritle cheered. "You've got to win that money for Pops!"

The clash of gears got Speed's blood pumping as he thundered down the track. Duggery was in his sights now.

Duggery contacted him on his radio.

"I should say thanks for saving me from that volcano, Speed, but the way I see it, we're even," Duggery said. "I wouldn't have gotten into that mess if those goons weren't after you. See you at the finish line, loser!"

Speed gritted his teeth and pressed the Mach 5 to go even faster. He hugged the next curve without slowing down at all. He had to get back to the head of the pack. The end of the race was coming up—on the same track where it started, in front of the crowd of racing fans.

Speed and Duggery easily zipped through

the competition, passing racer after racer. Soon an arch that looked like a giant wheel appeared in the distance—the gateway to the finish line.

"The leading cars are fast approaching the finish of the Sword Mountain Race!" the announcer told the crowd. "In just seconds, you'll see them rounding the final curve. Stand by!"

Excited fans stood in their seats, waiting for the finish. Down on the track, Pops paced back and forth. He had rushed to Sword Mountain as soon as he had recovered from Ace's attack. He was worried about his windshield, but he was worried about Speed even more.

"The first car coming down the home stretch is car number two, driven by Skull Duggery! And coming up fast is the Mach 5, driven by Speed Racer!" the announcer cried.

Pops brightened. "Speed's all right!"

He peered down the track. Duggery's red car and the Mach 5 came into view. Pops frowned when he saw the windshield.

"The windshield's been smashed!" he cried.

He was angry at first, but he was more relieved that Speed was all right.

Sure, those plans were on the windshield, Pops realized. *But that's not the only place I keep them . . .*

Speed and Duggery zoomed toward the finish line. The two cars were nose to nose. The crowd watched anxiously.

Who would win the race?

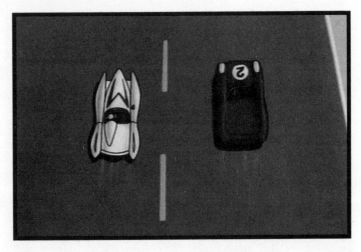

At the last second, Speed gunned the engine of the Mach 5. He slipped past Duggery at what looked like warp speed. Speed crossed the finish line a car's length ahead of his rival. The checkered flag at the finish line waved.

"The Mach 5 wins!" the announcer blared.

The fans in the stands burst into applause and cheers. Speed felt like he was dreaming. He had won his first race as a professional driver!

"I've won the money!" Speed said, barely believing it. "I can help Pops design the new engine for the Mach 5!"

Speed steered into the winner's circle and perched on top of the Mach 5. He watched the other racers finish, one by one. Sparky drove up last in his yellow car, with Trixie, Spritle, and Chim Chim in tow. They waved to Speed.

"Ladies and gentleman, the official winner is Speed Racer!" the announcer said.

Confetti rained down on Speed as the crowd chanted his name. Speed smiled and waved.

"Uh, just a moment, folks," the announcer interrupted. "Some bad news has just been handed to me. Due to the tactics and interference of a group of cars not officially entered, the results of the race have been canceled. There is no winner and no losers! I'm sorry, folks, but you'll just have to forget the whole thing!"

Speed was crushed. "I was counting on that money!"

Duggery's car was parked next to the Mach 5. He laughed. "Too bad. That was tough luck, Speed."

Pops stomped up to the car, followed by Trixie, Spritle, and Chim Chim. Pops looked pretty angry.

"Gee, I'm sorry, Pops, but if I hadn't smashed the windshield, those men would have gotten your design for the Mach 5 engine," Speed explained.

"It's all right," Pops said.

Speed was surprised. "Huh?"

Pops laughed. "I'm glad you broke it to protect the design, Speed, because I've got it right up here in my head."

Speed smiled with relief. "That's great, Pops!" Then a worried look crossed his face. "But how will you get the money now?"

Pops shrugged. "Don't worry about it, Speed. I'll think of something."

"You're a very clever man, Mr. Racer!" Trixie told him.

Spritle pulled on his pants leg. "And some of it's rubbed off on me, right, Pops?"

Pops had to think about this. "Hmmmm. Well, Spritle, I hope so."

"There's more prize money out there, Pops," Speed told him. "I intend to be the winner of the next race I'm in. You can count on it!"

"That's the way I like to hear you talk, Speed," Pops said. Then he froze. What had Speed just said? "The next race you're in? Hey, wait just a minute!"

Pops's face turned as red as his shirt. "Who gave you permission to be a racer, huh?" he bellowed.

Spritle and Chim Chim cried out at the sound of Pops's loud voice. A frightened Chim Chim jumped into Spritle's arms.

Then Pops got into lecture mode. He waved his fist in the air.

"It's very difficult to be a racer. It takes training and experience. Don't think because you won today that you've already become a professional racer," Pops went on. Spritle and Chim Chim silently copied his every move.

While Pops talked, Speed slowly shifted the Mach 5 into gear.

"That's enough lecture for now, Pops," Speed said cheerfully. He waved at his dad. Then he stepped on the gas. "See you later!"

"Speed!" Pops yelled.

Speed raced down the track. Pops ran to his car and hopped inside.

"Speed, you come back here!" he yelled. He raced down the track after his son.

Speed looked in his rearview mirror and laughed. Pops might be steamed now. But he knew in his heart that Speed had what it took to

be a great driver. All Speed had to do was prove it to him, and Pops would let him go pro.

"I'll show Pops I can handle it," Speed said. "Or my name isn't Speed Racer!"

SPEED'S BONUS RACE

During the race at Sword Mountain, Skull Duggery and I almost fell into a volcano. That was pretty dangerous! But Skull and I made it out alive.

That wasn't the last time I've been up close and personal with a volcano. Once, I entered a race on the mysterious island of Kapetopek. The race course wasn't like any course I'd ever experienced. The race started in a tunnel that cut right underneath a volcano and led to an abandoned underground city.

Not many racers could take the heat of such a tough race. A lot of drivers dropped out before the race even started. But I was ready for the challenge. I was racing against one of the world's greatest racers, Kabala, and I wanted to prove I could beat him.

Along the course I faced pools of boiling lava, a greedy racer out to steal the treasure of Kapetopek, and other dangers. Want to see if I made it across the finish line? Then rev your engine and get ready to read this bonus race!

BONUS RACE

Hour One

Speed Racer listened to the loud roar of the Mach 5's engine as he waited for the race to start. The heat of the volcano enveloped his body, but he tried to ignore it. He had to focus.

Chief Zuma, the ruler of Kapetopek, had opened the island's borders for the race. The League of Countries wanted Kapetopek to keep its borders open all the time, but Chief Zuma was against it.

To settle the matter, he had agreed to the race. Chief Zuma would pit the island's best racer, Kabala, against the finest racers from around the world. If Kabala lost, Chief Zuma would have to obey the League of Countries.

The League was counting on Speed to win. He didn't want to let them down.

Speed made a mental note of the drivers lined up next to him. On his right he spotted Mr. Kadar's red car. He knew Mr. Kadar was in the race for only one reason—to steal the treasure of the Kapetopeks. Mr. Kadar had brought a bunch of drivers in red cars to help ensure his win. Speed frowned. It was going to feel good to beat Mr. Kadar.

Way down on the left he saw Kabala's black car. The mysterious driver had a reputation as the world's greatest racer—and the most dangerous. Kabala's opponents always crashed before they finished the race. Was Kabala up to no good? No one had ever proven it.

Speed scanned the rest of the cars. He didn't see Racer X, the masked racer. Speed had talked to Racer X when Chief Zuma welcomed the drivers to the island. But now Speed didn't spot his car.

Must have dropped out, Speed guessed. *That's funny. That's not like Racer X at all.*

The ground beneath the cars began to rumble. Chief Zuma raised his staff.

"When the tunnel opens, the race will begin!" he cried. "Whatever man makes it through this terrible tunnel will be declared the greatest racer in the world!"

Speed kept his eyes on the rock wall in front of him. The rumbling got worse, almost like an earthquake. Then the rock wall began to slide open, as though it were being pushed by giant invisible hands.

"Start!" Chief Zuma yelled.

Speed raced forward. Hot steam poured from the inside of the tunnel. Rocks fell from the tunnel ceiling, smashing onto the floor.

Up ahead, Speed saw a river of lava flowing down the tunnel floors, blocking the path. There had to be some way across. There was a small path on the right side. If he could just ride up the tunnel wall a little, he'd make it.

Speed carefully steered toward the bubbling orange river. Then, suddenly . . .

Slam! Another car banged into the right side of the Mach 5, sending him spiraling out of control. Speed saw the laughing face of Mr. Kadar as he struggled to straighten out the car.

He screeched to a stop just in time. Another inch, and the lava would have engulfed him.

"Whew!" Speed said. But he wasn't out of danger yet. Another wave of lava poured down the right side of the tunnel—headed right for him! He had to get out of there, fast.

Speed stepped on the gas, but his back tires were stuck in a rut on the tunnel floor. He thought quickly and pressed the D button on the steering wheel.

A clear deflector extended over the cockpit, sealing Speed safely inside. The lava splattered on top of the deflector, sliding off harmlessly.

Then Speed hit the A button. Hydraulic jacks sprung from the bottom of the car. Speed used them to hop over the lava river.

Thanks to Mr. Kadar, Speed had lost some time and was now at the back of the pack. Speed pressed down on his gas pedal and zoomed through the tunnel.

Hour Two

As Speed raced on, he saw one of the cars crash into the side of the tunnel. Farther down, he saw another wreck.

Probably Mr. Kadar, Speed guessed. *He sabotaged them just like he tried to sabotage me.*

Speed shook his head, puzzled. Kabala was the one with the bad reputation. But Mr. Kadar was the one proving to be the most trouble.

A strange sight up ahead caused Speed to slow down. The drivers had all gotten out of their cars. They seemed to be staring at something.

Speed stopped the Mach 5 and joined them. A huge underground lake blocked their way. There was no way to get across.

"We'll have to turn back," Mr. Kadar was saying.

"Mr. Kadar," Speed said. "Did you happen to see that crash back there?"

"So you think I caused it?" Mr. Kadar replied, raising an eyebrow. "Well, good luck proving it!"

Mr. Kadar laughed loudly. His henchmen joined in. But another sound soon drowned them out.

The lake waters began to churn. A giant whirlpool spun around and around. The sound of the swirling waters echoed through the tunnels.

Speed watched as the water drained from the lake, almost as if someone had pulled a plug in the bottom. As the waters receded, something emerged from the lake's bottom.

"*Aaaaaah!*" The drivers screamed as the large gray head of a sea monster appeared. The monster had glowing eyes, sharp white teeth, and a horn rising from its snout.

Speed jumped back. As the rest of the monster's body came into view, Speed could see that it had four sturdy dinosaur-like legs supporting its massive belly. On the other side of the lake bed, Speed could see an opening to the rest of the tunnel.

I've got to get to the tunnel, Speed told himself. *But how am I supposed to get past a monster?*

The monster's long neck began to lean forward. With a sudden lurch, the neck broke off, sending sprays of rocks and dust over the racers.

Speed gasped as he looked at the broken head on the side of the lake.

"It was stone!" he cried. He jumped back into the Mach 5.

Kabala was quicker. He raced underneath the belly of the stone monster. Mr. Kadar and his goons quickly followed.

Speed zoomed right behind them. Above him, the giant stone monster began to shake and crumble once more. Rocks fell on all sides. He expertly steered, avoiding them.

Soon the mouth of the tunnel came into view. Speed breathed a sigh of relief as he entered it. Behind him, he heard a horrible crash as the stone monster came tumbling down.

Just in time, Speed thought.

Hour Three

Speed raced through the underground tunnel. The walls and ceiling of this part of the tunnel were made of dusty red rock. Strange-looking trees and flowers grew on all sides. Speed had never seen anything like them before.

"It's a petrified forest," Speed realized.

"Everything is made of stone!"

Suddenly Speed saw that one of the stone trees had toppled over, blocking the road. He hit the A button on his steering wheel, activating the hydraulic jacks.

Whoosh! Speed jumped over the logs. He landed safely on the other side.

Behind him, he heard a crash. He looked into his rearview mirror. Another driver hadn't been as lucky as Speed. He'd slammed right into the log!

Speed raced on. Up ahead, Mr. Kadar and his men had stopped their cars.

The petrified forest gave way to a dark tunnel. Glittering diamonds stuck out of the walls and ceiling, shining like stars. Mr. Kadar ordered his men to get the diamonds.

"There are enough diamonds here to make me the richest man in the world!" Mr. Kadar cried.

The grumbling henchmen obeyed. Chief Zuma had warned against stealing the Kapetopek treasure. Was it really cursed?

Abandoning the race, the men chiseled into the stone, trying to extract the diamonds. Mr. Kadar grinned. The diamonds in the tunnel were worth a fortune.

Then an ear-splitting scream made him turn. A horrible-looking creature hung from the ceiling. The giant monster had a pulsating pink body and a tangle of long orange tentacles. One of the tentacles reached down and wrapped around the

waist of one of Kadar's drivers. Another tentacle grabbed one of Kadar's race cars. Then the monster slammed both of them against the ground.

Mr. Kadar didn't even try to help. He jumped into his car and raced off. The other henchmen followed.

Speed zoomed up a few seconds later. He gasped when he saw the giant creature blocking his path. It looked like a strange cross between a plant and an insect.

Speed knew just what to do. He hit the C button on his controls. Two rotating saws extended from the front of the Mach 5. They sliced through the tentacles like they were blades of grass.

Speed drove further through the glittering tunnel. His heart pounded. What other dangers awaited him there?

Hour Four

Speed found out quickly enough. The dark tunnel led to an underground chamber. The road passed through a temple made of crumbling stone. Stone pillars held up the roof of the temple. Unusual markings were carved into the stone.

Speed would normally never slow down during a race, but he had to stop. He knew he'd never see a sight like this again. Around the temple were piles and piles of treasure—gold pieces, jewels, bowls, and other glittering

objects. Even in the darkness of the tunnel they gleamed brightly.

Speed was admiring the treasure when he heard a noise.

"Get back!" someone yelled. "This treasure belongs to the Kapetopeks!"

Speed peered around a tunnel column. Kabala was blocking a pile of treasure from Mr. Kadar and several of his men. Kabala wore a black jumpsuit over his tall, muscular body. The front of his black helmet was a mask that

extended down over his nose, covering most of his face.

Mr. Kadar held a heavy gold staff with a sharp, pointed diamond at the end. Speed guessed he had stolen it from one of the treasure piles. He pointed it threateningly at Kabala. But the racer did not seem worried.

"I'm here to protect the treasure," Kabala said firmly.

Mr. Kadar raised the staff over his head. Speed quickly grabbed a heavy jewel from a nearby pile of treasure. He hurled it at the staff, knocking it from Mr. Kadar's hands.

Mr. Kadar turned and glared at Speed angrily. "So it's you!"

"Sorry I interrupted," Speed replied.

"You're really going to be sorry now, Speed Racer," Mr. Kadar cried. "Get him!"

The two henchmen lunged at Speed. He grabbed one of them by the arm and flipped him over. Speed easily deflected the second man with a blow to the chest.

But the first man quickly got back on his feet.

Bam! He pummeled Speed with a karate chop. Speed reacted with a karate kick that sent the thug flying.

Mr. Kadar attacked Speed next.

Speed let out a cry as he delivered a karate chop to Mr. Kadar that sent him flying against one of the stone pillars. Mr. Kadar grunted, then charged at Speed like a football linebacker.

Wham! He knocked Speed backward into a pile of treasure. He wrapped his hands around Speed's neck. Speed quickly reacted with a strong kick. Mr. Kadar went tumbling back onto the temple floor.

Angry, Mr. Kadar reached for the sharp staff that Speed had kicked out of his hands before. But before he could grab it, Kabala stepped on his hand.

"Ow!" Mr. Kadar cried.

Kabala picked Mr. Kadar up by the front of his jumpsuit and hurled him out of the temple. The force of the throw loosened Kabala's mask, which fell to the temple floor.

Speed gasped. There was another mask underneath, around the driver's eyes. But Speed knew that face. "Racer X!" he cried. "What are you doing here?"

"Look out!" Racer X cried.

Speed turned to see one of the henchmen running toward him with a wrench in his hand. He flipped the thug, slamming him into the temple floor.

Mr. Kadar was back on his feet. "We have you outnumbered," he said. "There's no way you can win. We're taking the treasure, whether you like it or not."

Suddenly, the underground chamber began to rumble. Speed felt the stones move beneath his feet. Before he could run, the temple floor gave way!

Speed's stomach lurched as he fell into the emptiness underneath the temple. He braced for the impact as his body thudded into the dirt.

When he got to his feet, he saw that Racer X had fallen, too. Mr. Kadar and his thugs stood on top of the pit, laughing.

"Now we can take as much of the treasure as we want!" Mr. Kadar cried.

Hour Five

Speed and Racer X looked around the dark pit. The walls were too steep and high to climb. They stood there, helplessly, as they heard Mr. Kadar and his men loading the treasure into their race cars. Then the heard the sound of car engines speeding away.

"Sounds like they're gone," Speed said. "There's got to be another way out of here. Let's look."

"Good idea," Racer X agreed.

It was nearly impossible to see in the tunnel. They carefully walked ahead. They didn't get far when they saw stone steps leading out of the tunnel.

They climbed up the steps and found themselves on the other side of the temple. They walked across the stone floor back to their cars.

"Racer X, why did you disguise yourself as Kabala?" Speed asked.

"I'll tell you," Racer X replied. "I first met Kabala a few years ago. He taught me how to drive mountainous roads. Every racer was afraid of Kabala, but he was kind and helpful to me. He taught me special techniques that only he knew.

"And then, when I became a professional racer, I raced against Kabala," Racer X continued. "Suddenly, before he had a chance to avoid it, there was a landslide and his car fell into the valley below. I searched for him, but I never saw him again."

Racer X reached down and picked up Kabala's mask. He put it back on his face.

"To return his kindness, I disguised myself as Kabala so I could protect the treasure of the Kapetopeks," Racer X explained.

"And to protect the island's borders?" Speed asked.

"That's right," Racer X said. "If you win this race, the borders of Kapetopek will be open to any country in the world. Kapetopek will be ruined."

"That doesn't make sense!" Speed replied. "Kapetopek can't stay isolated from the world forever. It's a beautiful island. The world should see it."

"Please, Speed," said Racer X. "Drop out of the race. Do it for the people of Kapetopek."

Speed felt a little angry now. He wasn't a quitter. And he wasn't about to drop out of a race just because Racer X wanted him to.

"I'm racing to win," Speed said, walking away. "That's all. There's nothing you can say that will stop me."

"Speed! Come back here!" Racer X called out.

But Speed didn't listen. He ran to the Mach 5 and jumped in. As he sped off, he heard Racer X behind him.

Speed zoomed through the tunnel. He checked his odometer. The finish line was only a mile away. He stepped on the gas.

Then he saw what looked like a pile-up ahead. He reluctantly slowed down. The tunnel was blocked by another boiling river of lava. Red race cars stuck out of the lava, and they were sinking fast. Mr. Kadar's henchmen climbed up the walls of the cave, watching their cars sink. Mr. Kadar stood on the hood of his car, stuffing treasure into his pockets.

"My beautiful treasure! Gone!" he wailed.

Speed grinned. It served that villain right. He hit the A button on his controls. Then he used his hydraulic jacks to jump clear over the lava lake.

"See you later, Mr. Kadar!" he called out, waving.

Racer X was right behind him. He used one of the sinking cars as a ramp and cleared the lava in one jump.

The tunnel widened as the end of the course came into sight. Racer X sped up until he was right next to Speed.

Speed tried to speed up, but there just wasn't enough time. The two cars zipped through the tunnel exit at exactly the same time!

"It's a tie!" Chief Zuma cried.

The head of the League of Countries stood next to him. "Well, then Kapetopek must open its borders."

"Never!" cried Chief Zuma. "Our racer was not defeated."

Racer X climbed out of his car. He took off Kabala's mask. Everyone gasped.

"I risked my life to save your treasure," he told Chief Zuma. "You two must come to some agreement."

Chief Zuma nodded. "I see that you are right. Perhaps Kapetopek can open its borders some of the time."

Everyone cheered. Speed smiled.

He liked to win. But if he had to tie with any driver, he was glad it was Racer X!

SPEED RACER
THE NEXT GENERATION ™

**Racing to DVD
May 2008**

**Classic Speed Racer DVDs
Also Available!**